Yikes! Bikes!

Ready, Freddy!

Yikes! Bikes!

by ABBY KLEIN

illustrated by
JOHN MCKINLEY

THE BLUE SKY PRESS
An Imprint of Scholastic Inc. • New York

To Sydney and Jordan:
two of the coolest kids I know.
You're the best!
—A. K.

THE BLUE SKY PRESS

Text copyright © 2006 by Abby Klein
Illustrations copyright © 2006 by John McKinley
All rights reserved.

Special thanks to Robert Martin Staenberg.

SCHOLASTIC, THE BLUE SKY PRESS, and associated logos are
trademarks and/or registered trademarks of Scholastic Inc.
Library of Congress catalog card number: 2005015777
ISBN-13: 978-0-439-78456-6 / ISBN-10: 0-439-78456-5
21 20 19   12 13
Printed in the United States of America   40
First printing, February 2006

CHAPTERS

I have a problem.

A really, really, big problem.

I'm the only one in my class

who doesn't know how to ride

a two-wheeler, and I only have

two weeks to learn how!

Let me tell you about it.

CHAPTER 1

Doggy Days

"Boys and girls, I'd like to introduce you to Jo," said our teacher, Mrs. Wushy. "She works at the local animal shelter, and I invited her here today to talk to you about pet care. It looks like she brought along a furry friend of hers to meet you."

"Hello, everyone," said Jo. "My name is Jo, and this is Mickey. He's one of the dogs we have at the shelter right now who is looking for a good home. The shelter is a place where we take care of animals who got lost, ran away, or whose owners didn't want them anymore. It's my job to find them a new home."

"Oh, he's cute," said Jessie. "I wish I could take him home, but I'm not allowed to have any pets in my apartment."

"I'm not allowed to have any either," I said. "I live in a house, but my mom's such a Neat Freak, she won't let me have any pets, except my goldfish, Mako."

"Well, pets are a big responsibility," said Jo. "They take a lot of work. Can anyone tell me one thing you have to do to take care of a dog like Mickey?"

Robbie was the first one to raise his hand.

Robbie is my best friend, and he knows

a lot about taking care of pets because he has a gecko, a python, and a mouse. He practically has a whole zoo at his house. *His* mom doesn't mind the smell. "You have to feed a pet every day," Robbie said.

"That's right," said Jo. "You have to make sure your pet is not only getting *enough* food, but the right kind of food, as well. Good food makes your pet's coat shiny and gives your pet lots of energy to play. Very good comment. What else do you think you need to do for your pets?"

"Clean up its poop!" Max yelled out.

"Max," said Mrs. Wushy, "if you have something to say, please raise your hand. Do not just yell out."

"Max has a good point," Jo continued. "In fact, it is the law that you must clean up after your pet. If you take your dog for a walk, make sure you have something to use to pick up after him."

"Pooper scooper, pooper scooper," Max blurted out.

"Max, this is your last warning," said Mrs. Wushy. "If you call out one more time, then you will have to go sit in a chair."

Chloe's hand shot up, and she almost poked me in the eye with her painted red fingernails. "Oh, I know something that's really important," she said. She thinks *everything* she says is important. It's so annoying!

"Yes, honey, what is it?" Jo asked.

"All dogs have to go to the beauty parlor."

"You mean the groomer, Dumb-Dumb," Max said, snickering. "Dogs don't go to the beauty shop."

"Did you hear what he just called me?"

Chloe whined. "Mrs. Wushy, I think he should have a time-out."

"Chloe, you are not the teacher. You worry about yourself. It is *my* job to take care of Max, not yours."

"Anyway," Chloe continued, "I take my dog, Princess, to the beauty parlor every week. They give her a bath, comb out her

fur, and tie up her hair in little pink bows so it looks just like mine!"

"I think I'm gonna puke," I whispered to Robbie.

"Pets do need baths just like humans," Jo said. "You don't have to take them to a groomer, though. You can give them a bath right in your own bathtub."

"EWWW, that is so gross," said Chloe, wrinkling up her nose. "I wouldn't want to take a bath in the same tub as my dog. I'd get doggie cooties!"

"I think it's the other way around," Robbie whispered to me. "That poor dog would get cooties from *her*!" We burst out laughing.

"Freddy and Robbie, is there something you'd like to share with the class?" asked Mrs. Wushy.

"Oh no," we answered, biting our lips and trying not to laugh.

"Is there anything else you think is important?" Jo asked, trying to get us back on track.

Jessie raised her hand. "Exercise," she said. "Pets need to run around and play. I know I go crazy if I can't go out and play."

"Very good," said Jo. "Exercise makes pets happy and healthy. You can take your dog for a walk or play ball with him. That way, you both get exercise!"

"Well, boys and girls, it's almost time for Jo to go," said Mrs. Wushy, "but before she leaves, she has a very special event to tell you all about."

"Is it a dog show? Is it a dog show?" Chloe asked excitedly. "I just know my little Princess will come in first place."

"No, it's not a dog show," said Jo. "It's a Bike-a-thon. We are trying to raise money to care for the animals in the shelter until they are adopted. Here's how it works. We will have a bicycle course set up, and each time you ride around the course, that counts as one lap. You will have one hour to ride as many laps as you can. If you are

interested, take this sponsor sheet home and ask your friends and family to pay you for each lap you ride. Whatever money you raise will go to support the animals in the shelter."

"That sounds like fun," said Jessie.

"It is a lot of fun," answered Jo. "Just raise your hand if you're interested, and I'll give you one of these forms."

Everyone's hand shot up.

"Great! I look forward to seeing every-body two weeks from Saturday," Jo said as she passed out the papers. She put Mickey's leash on and started to head out the door. "Good-bye, everybody. Thank you so much for letting me come."

"Woof, woof!" Mickey barked.

"He says, 'See you on Saturday,' too!"

CHAPTER 2

Wanna Bet?

That day at lunch everyone was talking about the Bike-a-thon.

"I can't wait," said Chloe. "It's going to be so much fun! I'm going to ride my brand-new bike."

"Let me guess," said Jessie. "It's pink."

"It is," said Chloe. "How did you know?"

"Oh, just a lucky guess," Jessie answered, smiling at me.

"Anyway, it's got this adorable basket with flowers on it, and rainbow-colored ribbons that hang from the handlebars, and the funniest horn you ever heard that's shaped like a butterfly."

"Sounds perfect," Jessie said, turning to me and pretending to gag.

"I know," Chloe replied, fluffing her bouncy, strawberry-blonde curls.

"Of course you know," I muttered under my breath. "You know everything!"

"Well, my bike isn't new," said Jessie, "but I can ride really fast, so I will be able to do a lot of laps and raise lots of money for the animals."

"I bet you're as fast as a mako shark," I said. "They can swim as fast as 22 miles per hour."

"You're not that fast," Max snorted. "I bet I'm faster than you. Everybody knows boys are faster than girls."

"Says who?" Chloe asked, sticking her nose right into Max's face.

Max's eyes got big. "Are you talking to me?" he asked, slowly raising his fist.

"Uh, no," Chloe whispered as she quickly shrank back in her seat.

"Boys are not faster than girls, you big bully," Jessie said. "I bet I could beat you any day."

"Oh really?" Max said, laughing. "You think you're so tough. Well then, let's make a bet. I bet you your snack for a whole week that I will be able to ride more laps than you in the Bike-a-thon."

"You're on!" Jessie shot back.

"How about you, wimp?" Max turned to me and poked me in the chest. "You want to bet, too, Shark Boy? Oh, wait, what am I saying? You can't be in the Bike-a-thon. You have to ride a two-wheeler to do it, and you don't know how."

"Oh yes I do," I said, sticking out my chest and trying to sound convincing.

"Since when did the little baby learn to ride a two-wheeler?" Max snickered. "The last time I saw you out on your bike, it had training wheels on it."

"Well, maybe you need glasses to help you see better, because my bike doesn't have training wheels anymore!"

"Freddy's a liar, liar, pants on fire!" Max started singing loudly.

"I am not a liar!" I yelled back. "I guess you'll just see for yourself at the Bike-a-thon," I said, and I took another bite of my baloney sandwich.

Just then Robbie kicked me under the table, and I choked. Pieces of baloney sandwich almost came flying out of my nose. I turned to Robbie and whispered, "Hey, what are you doing?"

"The question is what are *you* doing?" Robbie whispered back. "You don't know how to ride a two-wheeler. That's a lie."

"Leave me alone. I know what I'm doing." I turned to Max. "OK, Max, I'll make you a bet, but I am not going to bet against Jessie. I know she's much faster than all of us."

Jessie smiled.

"Well then, what's the bet, Shark Bait?" Max asked, leaning in close to my face. I could feel his hot breath on my neck. My heart was pounding. I rubbed my shark's tooth for good luck.

"I bet that I can ride more laps than *you* at the Bike-a-thon."

"You? Ride more laps than me?" Max laughed. "That's a good one."

"No, I'm serious. Are you going to bet me or not?" I asked, trying to make my voice sound tough.

"It's a bet. Wait, what are we betting?"

"Same as you bet Jessie. Snack for a week," I said.

"You go, Freddy!" Jessie pumped her fist in the air. "You can do it!"

"Fine. It's a bet!" Max said.

"Let's shake on it," I said, sticking my hand out. He grabbed my hand and started squeezing so hard I thought it was going to break, but I didn't make a face.

"I can't believe you just did that," Robbie whispered. "I think you've lost your mind."

After that, I couldn't eat anymore because I was about to lose my lunch.

CHAPTER 3

Suzie's Big Mouth

That night at dinner my sister, Suzie, had to open up her big mouth.

"Hey, Mom, Dad, guess what? Today I heard that the animal shelter—"

Suzie didn't even get the whole sentence out of her mouth before my Neat Freak mom interrupted her. "The animal shelter! Stop right there," my mom said. "I don't think I like the sound of this. You both know I don't want any pets that shed or smell in this house."

"Oh, I know. Believe me, Mom, I know. But this isn't about adopting a pet. The shelter is going to have a Bike-a-thon in two weeks to raise money for the animals. Can I do it?"

"I think it's a great idea," my mom said. "Of course you can, Suzie, as long as you don't bring any furry friends home with you afterward."

"How about you, Freddy?" my dad asked. "Are you going to do it, too?"

Before I could even answer, Suzie piped up, "He can't."

"What do you mean he can't? Of course he can," my mom said, smiling.

"Oh no, he can't. You have to know how to ride a two-wheeler, and the little baby

still has to use training wheels," Suzie said, pretending to suck her thumb.

"I am not a baby!" I yelled.

"Oh, Freddy, don't let Suzie get you so upset," my mom said. "Just ignore her."

Easy for her to say.

"Are you sure that you can't use a bike with training wheels?" my dad asked.

"Fine. You don't believe me, then I'll get the entry form and show you," Suzie said, running out of the room. Seconds later she was back. She shoved the paper in my dad's face. "See for yourself, Dad," she said, poking at the paper. "It says right here that only two-wheelers are allowed."

"Slow down, Suzie," my dad said. "I can't read it when you're shaking it around like that. May I have the paper for a moment, please?" My dad read the note silently and then looked up at me. "I guess Suzie is right, champ. No training wheels. Only two-wheelers."

"Told you so!" Suzie said, grinning.

"Told you so. Told you so," I mimicked. "Why do you have to be such a brat all the time?"

"Why do you have to be my brother?" Suzie shot back.

"For your information, Miss Know-It-All, I am going to do the Bike-a-thon."

"Oh really? How?"

"I'm going to ride a two-wheeler."

"That's the funniest thing I ever heard," Suzie said, laughing. "There's no magic spell for learning to ride a bike. Do you think you are just going to wave your magic wand, and then *presto*, you'll be a pro like Lance Armstrong?"

"Duh. Don't you think I know that?"

"OK, OK, enough, you two," my dad interrupted. "Freddy, I'm a little confused. What do you mean when you say you're going to ride a two-wheeler?"

"I told everyone at school that I was going to, so I have no choice!" I answered.

"Why would you do a thing like that, honey?" my mom asked. "You know very well you can't, so why would you say that you could?"

"I didn't want them all to think I was a baby!" I said, sniffling. "Everybody already knows how to ride a two-wheeler by now.

Well, everybody except me. I'm so scared that I will fall off and break my arm. I already broke my arm once. I don't ever want to do that again. That was horrible." I wiped my nose on my sleeve.

"Oh, now look. The little baby-waby is crying," said Suzie.

"Not another word out of you, Suzie," my dad barked, "or you're going to your room. Now be quiet."

"I'm sure we can figure something out, honey," my mom said, giving me a kiss on the cheek.

"Of course we can. It's easy," my dad said. "I'll just teach Freddy how to ride a two-wheeler before the Bike-a-thon."

"Do you really think I can learn in just two weeks, Dad?"

"If you put your mind to it, you can learn anything," my dad said. "But you're going to have to work hard and practice, practice, practice."

"Oh, I'll practice all day if I have to."

"That's the spirit!" my dad said with a smile. "I like that attitude."

"Can we start now?" I asked, jumping up from the table. "Please, Dad, please?"

"I'm glad you're excited, but not tonight, Mouse. It's already dark. I'll tell you what. You get a good night's sleep, and we can start first thing in the morning since tomorrow is Saturday."

"Thanks, Dad. You're the best," I said, hugging him. "Get that wrench out, because tomorrow those training wheels are coming off!"

CHAPTER 4

Bye-Bye, Baby Bike

The next morning I was up at 5:00 A.M. Today was the big day. Today I was going to become a big kid. No more baby bike for me!

I put on my lucky shark underwear and the rest of my clothes and ran down to my parents' room to see if my dad was up yet. I tiptoed to his side of the bed and stared in his face. I could feel his breath on my cheek. All of a sudden his eyes flew open.

"AAAAHHHH!!!" he screamed. "Freddy, what are you doing? You scared the pants off of me!"

"I'm ready, Dad," I said, grinning from ear to ear.

"Ready for what?" my dad asked, rubbing his eyes and yawning.

"Ready to take those training wheels off my bike! Ready to ride like a big kid!"

"What time is it?"

"It's 5:05 A.M."

"Are you kidding me?" My dad groaned. "Freddy, it is way too early to go out bike riding. I'm going back to sleep."

"But how can you sleep on a day like this, Dad?" I asked as I started to pull off his covers. "We don't have any time to waste. Let's go, go, go!"

"Why don't you go, go, go back to your room and let me get a little more sleep," my dad said, rolling over.

"But Dad . . ."

"Freddy, if you don't let me get a little more sleep, then I won't take you out at all. Now go!"

"Oh, all right," I mumbled. "But if you're not up by 7:00 sharp, then I'll be back to get you."

"Good-bye," my dad grumbled and pulled the covers back over his head.

Two hours seemed like two years, but eventually my dad got out of bed and came downstairs for breakfast.

"Finally, Dad. I thought you were never going to get up! Are you ready to go?"

"Well, first I thought I might eat a little breakfast. I need some energy."

"Breakfast? We don't have time for breakfast, Dad. We've got to get out there now," I said, tugging on his shirt. "Let's go. You can eat later."

"Not so fast, Mouse," my dad said. "We all need to eat something first."

"That's right, Freddy," my mom said.

"You need some energy for your big day. How about some eggs and pancakes?"

"No, Mom, that takes too long. I'll just have a bowl of cereal."

"Now, Daniel, where are you going to take Freddy to practice?" my mom asked.

"Why don't you take him to the playground at school?" Suzie said. "That's where I learned to ride. It's actually a really good place because you can ride around on the field, and if you fall down, you don't get hurt. You just land in the grass."

"Oh no! Not the playground!"

"Why not?" Suzie asked.

"Because I told all my friends that I already knew how to ride a two-wheeler. I don't want any of them to see me there practicing. If Max found out the truth, he'd never stop calling me a baby."

"Well," said my dad, "let's see if we can think of any other places with big grassy areas like that."

I hit my forehead with the palm of my hand. "Think, think, think."

"What are you doing, weirdo?" Suzie asked. "Talking to yourself?"

"I'm trying to think of a good place to go. We're wasting time right now. Time I could be out there practicing!"

"Oh, I know," Suzie said, "how about the park near Papa Dave and Grammy Rose's house? I think it has a huge baseball field. I doubt anyone will be using it because it isn't baseball season."

I jumped up out of my chair, ran over to Suzie, and gave her a great big hug. "You're the best sister in the whole world!"

"I know," she said, smiling. "But can you let go now? You're squeezing my breakfast right out of me!"

"Oh, yeah, sure," I said. Then I grabbed my helmet and started running toward the door. "Come on, guys!" I called back to the kitchen. "What are you all waiting for? Let's go, go, go!"

CHAPTER 5

Eating Grass

We drove to the park near my papa and grammy's house. Suzie had come along, too, because she said she wanted to help. I think she just wanted to show off. We unloaded the bikes from the car, and Suzie hopped on hers and started riding while I walked mine. We headed over toward the field, and lucky for us, no one was using it.

"See? I told you this park had a big field," Suzie said in her know-it-all voice.

"Yes, it does," said my dad. "It's perfect for Freddy to practice on. Are you ready to get started, Mouse?"

"I think so," I answered, but my voice was shaking a little bit, and my stomach started doing some flip-flops. I wasn't so sure I could do this after all.

"Oh, is the little baby getting scared now?" Suzie said.

"Be quiet, brat!" I snapped at her. "Dad, why did you let her come?"

"Suzie," my dad began, "I let you come along because you said you wanted to help. That doesn't sound very helpful to me. We need to encourage Freddy and cheer him on. Do you think you can do that?"

"Whatever." Suzie shrugged and rode off.

"Good. I don't need her help anyway," I mumbled to myself.

"Now let's see," said my dad. "Freddy, why don't you put on your helmet, hop on your bike, and start pedaling. I'll hold the back of the bike until you get your balance, and then I'll let go."

"OK, Dad." I rubbed my lucky shark's tooth extra hard. "Here I go." I jumped on the bike and started pedaling. "Hey, this is easier than I thought."

"Hang on a minute, Sport," my dad called as he ran behind my bike. "Remember, I'm still holding the back. Do you think you're ready for me to let go?"

"Yeah, no problem, Dad! I got it! You can let go now!"

The next thing I knew, I landed face-first on the field, and my mouth was full of grass. As I tried to spit it out, I wondered how cows could eat this stuff. It tasted really gross.

My dad and Suzie came running over. "Freddy, Freddy, are you OK?" my dad asked, wiping grass off my face.

"Yeah, that was some wipeout," Suzie

said. "Too bad we didn't have the video camera. I think you did a flip right over the handlebars. We could have sent that one in to *America's Funniest Home Videos*!"

"I think I'm OK," I said. I started to get up, still spitting some of the grass and dirt out of my mouth. "Pfft, pfft, pfft, this grass tastes horrible."

"Unfortunately that's probably not the

last time you'll eat grass today," my dad said. "But you're tough. Now, let's try again, but this time keep looking straight ahead, and try not to turn the handlebars so much."

"And don't stop pedaling when Dad lets go," Suzie chimed in.

"I don't know if I can remember all that," I said.

"We'll remind you." My dad smiled. "Now hop on."

"What if I fall down again?"

"Oh, you'll fall down again," my dad said. "In fact, you'll fall down many more times today before you get the hang of it."

"Yeah, I must have fallen down about a gazillion times when I was learning to ride," added Suzie.

"Really?"

"Yep, really. At least you're on the grass, so it doesn't hurt too much."

"Come on, Freddy. Hop on," my dad said, patting the bike seat.

I got on and started pedaling. "Now this time when I let go," my dad continued, "remember to look straight ahead, and hold the handlebars steady."

"And don't forget to keep pedaling!" Suzie called after me.

"OK, I won't!"

"Get ready, Freddy. I'm letting go now," my dad said.

"OK!" *Look straight ahead, hold steady, keep pedaling*, I repeated over and over to myself. This time I think I pedaled about three times before I did a face-plant.

"That was better," said my dad. "But if you think you're going to crash, don't put

your foot down. That is not a good way to stop. You need to push back on the pedals to brake. That's the proper way to stop your bike."

We must have been out there practicing for at least two hours. I was starting to get the hang of it, but there was no way I was ready for the Bike-a-thon unless they decided to make it a Demolition Derby. "Aww, come on, Dad. Just a little bit more."

"Sorry, Freddy, but I'm exhausted. I just can't run anymore. We'll go practice again tomorrow. Don't worry. The big day is still two weeks away."

That may have seemed like a long time to him, but to me it was just around the corner, and I wasn't even close to ready. If I didn't ride in the Bike-a-thon, I might as well never show my face at school again!

CHAPTER 6

Pants on Fire

I had been practicing all weekend, but I still couldn't go very far before I fell off or crashed into something. Oh, why did I open my big mouth and make that stupid bet with Max anyway?

On Monday morning I put on long pants and a long-sleeved shirt, so no one would see my cuts and bruises. When I got on the bus, all the kids were talking about the Bike-a-thon, of course.

Chloe was bragging, as usual. "I've already started getting sponsors for the Bike-a-thon. My nanna said she'd give me one hundred dollars for every lap I ride. Did you all hear that? One hundred dollars!"

"Whoop-dee-doo for you," I muttered under my breath.

"Sit down and shut up, you big bragger," said Max. "You think you're so wonderful. Well, guess what? You're not!"

Robbie and I started to laugh. "I can't believe he just said that to her," Robbie whispered.

"Yeah, it was hilarious! Did you see the look on Chloe's face when he told her to shut up?"

"Ooohhh, you're so mean, Max Sellars," Chloe scolded, her strawberry-blonde curls bouncing wildly. "Just wait until we get to

school. I'm going to tell Mrs. Wushy what you said to me, and you're going to be in big, big trouble!"

"Oh, I'm so scared," Max said, pretending to shiver.

Chloe plopped back down in her seat to pout, and then the fun was over because Max turned to me.

"So, Freddy, are you getting ready for the big day?" Max said, grinning.

"Oh, I'm ready," I said, trying to swallow over the lump in my throat. Who was I kidding? I wasn't even close to ready. He was going to kick my butt.

"Really? I can't wait to beat the pants off of you and Jessie. I can just taste those extra snacks right now!" Max said, licking his fat lips.

"Not so fast," Jessie interrupted. "You

won't be getting my snack or Freddy's. In fact, you're going to be sorry you ever made the bet. Right, Freddy?" Jessie said, turning to me.

"Uh, yeah. Right," I said, smiling weakly. This was not going very well. The whole bus was staring at me. I had to say something to sound tough. "Max, you may scare

some people, but you don't scare me and Jessie. We're going to kick your butt on Saturday, Mister!" As soon as the words were out, I wished I could take them back, but I couldn't. They were out there, and the whole bus had heard them.

There was a chorus of *ooooohs* from all the kids.

Jessie patted me on the back and yelled, "You go, Freddy!"

"Yeah, in your dreams. You think you're so tough? Well, you'll never beat me," Max snickered, and he sat back down in his seat.

Just then Robbie elbowed me in the ribs. "Now you've really lost your mind," he whispered. "How in the world are you going to beat Max Sellars?"

"I don't know," I whispered, shaking my head. "I don't know. I think I need a miracle."

"Maybe I can help," Robbie whispered back. "I'm not a miracle worker, but I have an idea. I'll come over after school and teach you a little trick."

"You're the best friend a guy could have," I said, giving his arm a squeeze. "The best!"

CHAPTER 7

The Trick

That day after school, Robbie came over to my house to help me out.

"OK, where's the magic potion?" I asked hopefully.

"Magic potion? What are you talking about?" said Robbie.

"You said you had a trick, and since you're totally into science, I thought maybe you made some special potion with your chemistry set that would magically turn me into a bike-riding superstar."

"Sorry, no potion. I'm a scientist, not a wizard. Besides, we don't need magic," said Robbie. "When I said 'trick,' I meant a little something my dad taught me when I was learning to ride a two-wheeler."

"Oh," I mumbled, trying hard to hide my disappointment.

"Come on, Freddy. It's not that bad," Robbie said, patting me on the back.

"Maybe not for you. You weren't stupid enough to make a bet with the biggest bully in the whole first grade. I'm never going to be able to ride in that Bike-a-thon. I will always just be a baby with a baby bike. Little Baby Freddy."

"Now you *are* sounding like a baby," said

Robbie. "Stop whining, and go get your bike so we can get started."

I went to the garage and came back with my helmet and my bike.

"All right," Robbie began. "Here's the trick. Once you start riding, do not look down at your feet. The minute you start to look down, the handlebars turn, and you lose your balance. Just keep looking straight ahead. Your feet know what to do. You don't need to check on them."

"That's it? That's your special trick?" I said, shaking my head. "Are you kidding me? That will never work."

"Trust me. It works," Robbie said. "Just try it. What have you got to lose?"

"My snack for a week. That's what I've got to lose!"

"Here. Watch me. I'll go first," Robbie said. He put on my helmet, hopped on my bike, and rode down to the end of the block and back perfectly. And he never looked down once. "OK, now it's your turn," he said.

"Fine, but I don't think it's going to make any difference. Be prepared to watch me fall. No laughing when I crash. Deal?"

"Deal. Now get going already. And remember, don't look at your feet!"

I put on my helmet and climbed on my bike. "Keep a lookout for Max. I don't want him to see me practicing."

"I'll watch for Max. You just think about what I told you," Robbie said.

I got the pedals in place, and then I pushed off. I could feel my legs shaking a little bit, but I didn't look down.

I heard Robbie screaming, "Don't look down! Don't look down!"

I passed one house. Then the next. Then the next. "Don't look down," I whispered to myself. "Don't look down." I couldn't believe it. I was going much farther than I had ever gone before. Robbie's trick was working! I was so excited that I turned around to tell Robbie and crashed into a tree.

Robbie came running over. "Freddy, are you all right?"

"Yeah, I'm fine, thanks to this thing," I said, knocking on my helmet.

"You were awesome!" Robbie exclaimed, punching me on the shoulder.

"I know. I can't believe it!" I said, shaking my head. "I've never gone that far before. Your trick really does work."

"I told you so," Robbie said, smiling.

The two of us stayed out there practicing until it got dark, and each time I rode, I went farther and farther until I could ride down to the end of the block and back

without stopping. Just like a big kid. I was starting to think that maybe I could beat Max Sellars after all.

"Do you think I can do it?" I asked Robbie as we were walking my bike back to the garage.

"Do what?"

"Beat Max Sellars," I said. I parked my bike, put the kickstand down, and hung up my helmet.

"Yep, and I can't wait to see his face when he finds out you rode more laps than he did." Robbie chuckled.

"Me either! It's gonna be great! You're the best friend in the whole world," I said to Robbie, giving him a great big hug. "What would I ever do without you?"

"Let's hope we never have to find out."

Just then Robbie's mom pulled into the driveway to pick him up.

"Keep practicing, remember my trick, and we'll all beat Max at the Bike-a-thon," Robbie called as he hopped into the car.

I gave him two thumbs up as the car drove away. "Beat Max Sellars," I whispered to myself. "Beat Max Sellars."

CHAPTER 8

The Big Day

The day of the Bike-a-thon finally arrived. I had been practicing really hard every day after school. If I could beat Max, this would be the best day of my life. I would need all of my good luck charms: my lucky penny, my lucky shark underwear, *and* my lucky shark's tooth. I found the penny and my underwear with the great white sharks on it, but I could not find my lucky shark's tooth. I ran to look in the bathroom, but of course the door was locked. Suzie was in there trying to make herself look beautiful.

I banged on the door. "Hey, you big pain, let me in!"

"Go away, Stinkyhead! I'm busy!"

"You're not going to a ball. You're going to the Bike-a-thon! You don't need to make yourself all fancy," I yelled at her through the door.

Suzie made the mistake of unlocking the door so she could open it and yell in my face, but I pushed my way into the bathroom as soon as she opened it a crack. "Hey, what do you think you're doing, Mega Mouth?" she screamed.

"I'm trying to find my lucky shark's tooth. It's gotta be in here."

"You and that dumb shark's tooth!"

"For your information, it's not dumb,

and I *have* to have it today, or I will lose the bet for sure."

"What bet?"

Oh no! I can't believe I just said that in front of her. I decided to act as if I didn't hear her.

"What bet?" she asked again.

I kept my mouth shut.

"Hello. Earth to Freddy. I said, 'what bet?'" she asked for the third time. She was not going to let this one go.

"Oh, it's just some stupid bet I made with Max," I mumbled.

"I can't believe you made a bet. You are going to be in so much trouble when I tell Mom and Dad," Suzie said, smiling.

I grabbed her by the shoulders. "Please don't tell them," I pleaded.

"Well, what's in it for me?"

"How about if I make your bed for a whole week?"

"A whole week? You must really not want me to tell."

"Is it a deal?" I asked.

"I guess so," she said.

"Pinkie swear?" I asked, as we locked our pinkies.

"Pinkie swear," she said, nodding her head. "Oh, and by the way, your lucky shark's tooth is in the drawer right there. I just saw it when I was getting my brush."

I grabbed the shark's tooth and started running back to my bedroom. "Thanks!" I yelled over my shoulder. "You're the best sister in the whole world!"

"I know!" she called back.

When I was all dressed, I headed downstairs for breakfast.

"Well, look who's here," my mom said, smiling. "It's Lance Armstrong."

"Are you ready for the big day, Mouse?" my dad asked. "You have been practicing a lot. I think you're looking pretty good out there."

My mom came over and gave me a big

hug. "Oh, Freddy, you're getting to be such a big boy."

Now she was starting to get a little too gushy. "Uh, Mom, could you stop hugging me now? I can't breathe."

"Oh sorry, honey. It's just that I'm so proud of you."

"I think I'm going to be sick," Suzie said, rolling her eyes. "What's for breakfast?"

"You know champions need a good breakfast, so I made blueberry pancakes, scrambled eggs, and bacon," my mom said, placing heaping plates of food down in front of both of us.

"Yum," I said, licking my lips. "My favorite!" I started shoveling the food into my mouth.

"Slow down, honey," my mom said.

"You have plenty of time before the Bike-a-thon starts. You don't want to get cramps."

"I know. But I need a lot of energy because I have to ride a lot of laps today."

"Don't worry too much about how many laps you do," my mom continued. "The number of laps isn't the most important thing. You both got lots of sponsors. The

shelter will be grateful for any amount of money you raise to help the animals."

The total number of laps might not be important in her world, but in mine, it was everything! Beating Max was my ticket into the world of big kids. As far as I was concerned, this was going to be the last day that Max Sellars called me a baby!

CHAPTER 9

The Real Winner

As we drove over to the Bike-a-thon, my palms began to sweat. Oh no! What if they got so sweaty that they slipped right off the handlebars? That would be a disaster! I wiped them on my pants and took a few deep breaths.

"Freddy, are you OK back there?" my mom asked.

"Yeah, fine, Mom," I said, trying to sound confident. Although now that we were pulling up to the Bike-a-thon, and I could see Max standing there grinning, I thought I was going to throw up.

"Here we are," my dad said. "Let's unload the bikes so you two can get started."

We took the bikes out of the car and walked them over to where all the kids were waiting.

"Well, lookie here," Max said, snickering. "If it isn't Baby Freddy. Did you forget your tricycle?"

"Oh Max, that's so funny I forgot to laugh," I said.

"I wouldn't be laughing if I were you," Jessie said to Max. "Freddy and I are going to beat the pants off of you today. And

when that happens, *you'll* be crying like a baby." Then she turned to me and gave me a high five.

Jessie is so brave. I wish I could be more like her.

Just then Jo from the animal shelter

started giving us all instructions. "First of all, boys and girls, my furry friends and I want to thank you all for participating in the Bike-a-thon today. All the money we raise will help us take care of the animals until we can find them good homes. We have a course set up right over there," she said, pointing to the track, "and you're going to ride as many laps as you can in one hour. But remember, this is not a race. Just go out there and have fun."

Yeah, right. Not a race. This was going to be the most important race of my life! We all walked our bikes over to the starting line and put on our helmets.

Robbie pulled up next to me and whispered, "Good luck, Freddy. Just remember our little trick, 'don't look down.'"

"Thanks, Robbie. I'll be looking straight ahead the whole time, and Max will be looking at the back of my head," I said, laughing.

Jo gave the signal to go, and I hopped on my bike and took off. I had a great start, and I was feeling pretty good, but then Max whizzed right past me. He smiled and waved. "So long, sucker," he called.

"Oh no! This can't be happening," I thought. "I'm doomed. Whatever made me think I could beat Max Sellars?" My bike started to wobble a little bit. I was losing concentration. I was about to fall.

Then I heard a voice from behind me. "Come on, Freddy. You can do it. Show that big bully that you're not a baby." I smiled. I would know that voice anywhere.

It was Jessie. She was so fast, she was already coming around for her second lap.

I took a deep breath. This was my chance. I had to show Max that I wasn't a

baby. It was now or never. I started to pedal with all my might. "Don't look down," I whispered to myself. "Don't look down."

The next thing I knew, I was pulling up alongside Max. This time it was my turn to say, "So long, sucker!" And boy did it feel good! Max was so surprised, he almost fell off his bike.

"Hey, where did you come from, Shark Boy?" he called after me.

"Get a good look at me now," I yelled back, "because the next time you'll see me is at the finish line."

Then I took off riding as fast as I could. Max tried to catch up, but he just couldn't. From that point on, he never passed me again.

When it was all over, Jessie and Robbie

jumped off their bikes and came running over to me. Jessie hugged me and jumped up and down, yelling, "We did it! We did it!" Robbie gave me a high five and a slap on the back. "Way to go, Freddy!"

Max tried to sneak away, but Jessie grabbed him. "Hey, not so fast. We made a bet, remember? Freddy and I need to tell you what we want for snack on Monday." Then we all started laughing so hard that I thought we were going to pee in our pants.

Thanks to my two good friends, Jessie and Robbie, today was the best day of my life! Max could never call me a baby again. But the real winners were the animals. I rode a total of forty laps and raised fifty-two dollars for the animal shelter.

Now if I can just convince my mom to get me a dog. . . .

DEAR READER,

I am a dog freak. I have four dogs: Baxter, Camby, Sonny, and Mickey, and I love them all. Someday, I'd like to have ten dogs!

All of my dogs are adopted. They were rescued by my local animal shelter, and that is where I got them. If you and your family are thinking about getting a dog or a cat, you should think about going to your local animal shelter or SPCA. I'll bet you'll find a beautiful dog or cat just waiting for you to take him or her home.

I hope you have as much fun reading *Yikes! Bikes!* as I had writing it.

HAPPY READING!

Abby Klein

Freddy's Fun Pages

FREDDY'S SHARK JOURNAL

THE SPINY, OR PIKED, DOGFISH

They are the most common species of shark, and they are found in many places in the world.

The babies grow inside their mother for almost two years before they are born.

They have poisonous spikes or spines on their dorsal fins.

They live the longest of all sharks. They can live to be 70–100 years old!

FREDDY'S SECRET RIDDLE

Use the code below to find the answers to my riddles.
—Freddy

a	e	m	n	o	p
☺	*	☹	■	#	◆

r	s	t	u	v
@	→	$	●	⊙

What does a dog take when he goes camping?

How do you make a puppy disappear?

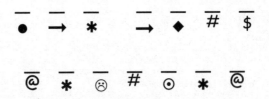

TANGLED LEASHES!

Chloe, Freddy, and Robbie are walking dogs to earn money. Help them figure out which dog they're walking.

_____'s dog _____'s dog _____'s dog

A VERY SILLY STORY
by Freddy Thresher

> Help Freddy write a silly story by filling in the blanks on the next two pages. The description under each blank tells you what kind of word to use. Don't read the story until you have filled in all the blanks!
>
> HELPFUL HINTS:
> A **verb** is an action word (such as run, jump, or hide).
> An **adjective** describes a person, place, or thing (such as smelly, loud, or blue).

When you first get a pet _____, you will
                              (type of animal)

need a _____ to put it in. It will also
      (piece of furniture)

need a _____ and a _____ to play with.
    (toy)   (another toy)

When your pet is hungry, give it lots of_____
                                      (food)

and_____. Feed it in a _____. Keep it
(something to drink)   (a thing)

clean by washing it with a_____ _____ .
                     (an adjective)   (thing)

Your pet will need a name, so try calling it

_____ . Say, "Here _____ , here
(person in room)   (same person)

_____ ," and see if your pet comes to you.
(same person)

You can dress it up. Put a _____ and
                          (article of clothing)

a _____ on it. You can dress up, too. For
(article of clothing)

more fun, put on your favorite _____ .
                               (article of clothing)

Exercise your pet. Take it to the _____ and let it
                                  (place)

_____ . You can use _____ treats to train
(verb)   (food)

it to _____ and _____ . When your pet
      (verb)   (verb)

_____ is happy, it will _____ and _____ .
(same animal)   (verb)   (verb)

If you _____ and _____ with it, your
       (verb)   (verb)

pet can be your best _____ friend.
                     (an adjective)

Have you read all about Freddy?

Freddy will do anything to lose a tooth fast!

Freddy's research turns up some unexpected results!

Freddy's found the best show-and-tell ever!

Can Freddy beat out Max the bully to join the hockey team?

Help! Does anyone have a magic spell for talent?

Can Freddy find a way to make the vampire go away?

Don't miss Freddy's next adventure!